For Cameron –

Poems for you,
And Mommy and Daddy, too!

Love,

Uncle Frank
and
Uncle Bill

Christmas 2000
Chicago

Climb INTO MY Lap

FIRST POEMS TO READ TOGETHER

SELECTED BY Lee Bennett Hopkins

ILLUSTRATED BY Kathryn Brown

SIMON & SCHUSTER BOOKS FOR YOUNG READERS

Contents

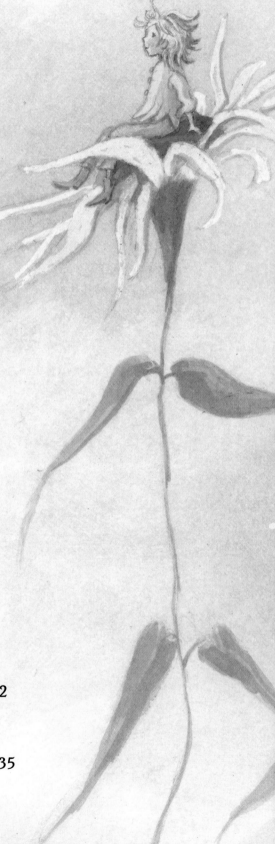

Introduction

One of the richest gifts we can give children is the gift of poetry. Toys, clothes, video games, and other material objects become worn, outgrown. But a little piggy going to market, an eentsy, weentsy spider climbing up a waterspout, and fairy folk frolicking linger in children's hearts and minds forever—and ever—especially when shared by adults whom they love.

But it *is* adults who must bring poetry to children—the father and mother who delight in moments spent with a son or daughter reading favorite selections; the grandparent who knows deep inside the profound impact poetry can breathe into young lives; the teacher, the librarian who introduces the world of poetry, brings it strong into children's hearts and minds.

I have long wanted to do a new book of poems that begged to be read, savored, jointly between adults and children, showing how poetry can evoke the warmth and comfort of togetherness.

Over a decade has passed since I compiled *Side by Side: Poems to Read Together*, a wondrous book to do, joyously illustrated by the incomparable Hilary Knight.

Since the publication of *Side by Side* I have been asked countless times for another. But to do "another" posed a great challenge. For the past several years I thought about and sought out poems for *Climb Into My Lap* centering around the specific needs and interests of younger children—to include works that invite participation, explore relationships between family, friends, and pets—to form a fresh concert for today's youth to experience.

As I did in *Side by Side*, I searched for a balance of the classics and the new to bring into youngsters' lives, perhaps for the first time, timeless voices of such writers as Lewis Carroll, Eugene Field, Edward Lear, as well as to introduce a bevy of work especially commissioned for this collection.

I want young children to hear, come to love, take to heart poems about their own immediate experiences—taking a bath, brushing their teeth, finding a special place to be alone with secret thoughts, losing themselves in worlds of make-believe, laughing and enjoying wordplay, discovering big thoughts that only poetry can give them in a few words and lines.

Poetry is magical, mystical, whimsical. Whether children are chuckling about being on top of spaghetti, meeting a mama who "hums a sea-song with her eyes," riding high on Daddy's shoulders, napping with Grandma, marveling over a Quangle Wangle's hat, or tongue tripping with a Jabberwock, youngsters can revel in poetic imagery.

It is thrilling to see how Kathryn Brown has interpreted and enhanced the poetry in this volume with fanciful, tender, loving, luminous illustrations. Her images and scenes beg to be looked at over and over again.

So—take this book on *your* lap—with a child.

Read and wander—wonder and ponder—delight and dream. Give children poetry— a gift from the past, a present for the future—words and thoughts and feelings they will remember, thank you for, their whole lives through.

—LEE BENNETT HOPKINS
Scarborough, New York

Me!

Quiet Morning

Early in the morning
dog, book and me
spend quiet moments
just we three.

Snuggled by the window,
chin on my knee,
close to the raindrops,
dog, book and me.

KAREN B. WINNICK

An Indignant Male

The way they scrub
Me in the tub,
I think there's
    Hardly
    Any
    Doubt
Sometime they'll rub
And rub and rub
Until they simply
    Rub
    Me
    Out.

A. B. Ross

See, I Can Do It

See, I can do it all myself
With my own little brush!
The toothpaste foams inside my mouth.
The faucet waters rush.

In and out and underneath
And round and round and round:
First I do my upstairs teeth
And then I do my down—

The part I like the best of it
Is at the end, though, when I spit.

DOROTHY ALDIS

My Name

I wrote my name on the sidewalk
But the rain washed it away.

I wrote my name on my hand
But the soap washed it away.

I wrote my name on the birthday card
I gave to Mother today

And there it will stay
For Mother never throws

ANYTHING

of mine away!

LEE BENNETT HOPKINS

Toy Telephone

FOR J.G.

When nobody's around to play with me
And I am all alone,
The thing I like the most to do
Is use my telephone.

I can talk to Grandma,
The astronauts, a ghost!
I can talk to anyone
I want to talk to most.

I talk and talk and talk and talk
Until I look to see,
My friend outside the window
Who'll *really* talk to me.

LEE BENNETT HOPKINS

11

Everybody Says

Everybody says
I look just like my mother.
Everybody says
I'm the image of Aunt Bee.
Everybody says
My nose is like my father's.
But *I* want to look like ME!

DOROTHY ALDIS

Tent

My skin is like
A canvas tent
That's stretched
From bone to bone;
It's cut to measure
Just for me,
I wonder where
It's sewn?
And why can't I
Unzip the front
And roam outside,
Then in?
But here I stay
Each night, each day,
Alone,
Within my skin.

DEBORAH CHANDRA

Secret Places

And There

When I want to—
When I'm ready—
I have a secret place
                      to go,

And there—
I'll sit
And think the thoughts
That no one else
                  should ever know.

Prince Redcloud

A Place of My Own

Sometimes I'd really like to be a troll.
I'd sit under my bridge and watch the whole
River bank, the water, and the sky.
Rocks and ducks and rushes would be my
Private kingdom, never shared with others
Like billy goats, grown-ups, or little brothers!

Fran Haraway

Alone

The woods,
The woods
Are deep and cool,
And there
The shadows
Play.

The woods,
The woods
Are just the place
To spend
This lazy summer
Day.

ANONYMOUS

The Secret Place

Halfway up a certain tree
There's a place belongs to me.
Two branches make a little chair
And I like sitting there.

I like it.
And it's secret too.
No grown-up guesses where I go.
And if he should, and climbed to it—
He would not fit, he would not fit!

DOROTHY ALDIS

18

This Is My Rock

This is my rock,
And here I run
To steal the secret of the sun;

This is my rock,
And here come I
Before the night has swept the sky;

This is my rock,
This is the place
I meet the evening face to face.

DAVID McCORD

Comfortable Old Chair

A bird has a nest
A fox has a lair
A den is home
If you're a bear.
I have a comfortable old chair.

Soft pillowed blue,
a flowered cloud.
The perfect place to read aloud
to myself or silently
letting long words run over me,
letting the stories I have read
make moving pictures in my head.
New chairs are nice
but mine is best.
My spot to think in
brood in
rest
to plot in
dream in, many dreams,
to scheme a few outlandish schemes in.
Kings need crowns to be the king
but me
I can be anything
any person
anywhere
if I just have my book and chair.

KARLA KUSKIN

My Secret Step

Tonight I should be upstairs.
Tonight I should be good.
But everyone is downstairs,
where I'd be if I could.

And so I'm in the middle,
between the up and down;
listening to the grown-ups talk,
but I don't make a sound.

The dishes clink,
my mother laughs,
the candles sparkle bright;
and I sit on my secret step

being good tonight.

REBECCA KAI DOTLICH

It's So Funny!

On Top of Spaghetti

On top of spaghetti, all covered with cheese,
I lost my poor meatball, when somebody sneezed.

It rolled off the table, and onto the floor,
And then my poor meatball, rolled out of the door.

It rolled into the garden, and under a bush,
And then my poor meatball, was nothing but mush.

The mush was as tasty, as tasty can be,
And early next summer, it grew into a tree.

The tree was all covered, with beautiful moss,
It grew lovely meatballs and tomato sauce.

So if you eat spaghetti, all covered with cheese,
Hold onto your meatball, and don't ever sneeze.

ANONYMOUS

23

Who Ever Sausage a Thing?

One day a boy went walking
And went into a store;
He bought a pound of sausages
And laid them on the floor.

The boy began to whistle
A merry little tune—
And all the little sausages
Danced around the room!

ANONYMOUS

A Young Farmer of Leeds

There was a young farmer of Leeds
Who swallowed six packets of seeds.
    It soon came to pass
    He was covered with grass,
And he couldn't sit down for the weeds!

ANONYMOUS

My Dog

I've got a dog as thin as a rail,
He's got fleas all over his tail;
Every time his tail goes flop,
The fleas on the bottom all hop to the top.

ANONYMOUS

How to Talk to Your Snowman

Use words that are pleasing,
Like: freezing
And snow,
Iceberg and igloo
And blizzard and blow,
Try: Arctic, Antarctic,
Say: shiver and shake,
But whatever you *never* say,
Never say: *bake.*

BEVERLY MCLOUGHLAND

Bursting

We've laughed until my cheeks are tight.
We've laughed until my stomach's sore.
If we could only stop we might
Remember what we're laughing for.

DOROTHY ALDIS

Some People

People

Some people talk and talk
and never say a thing.
Some people look at you
and birds begin to sing.

Some people laugh and laugh
and yet you want to cry.
Some people touch your hand
and music fills the sky.

CHARLOTTE ZOLOTOW

Mama's Song

Mama hums a sea-song with her eyes,
A deep blue rising sea-song,
    moving as her eyes move,
    weaving foam across my face.

White gulls whirl overhead,
The sun washes back and forth,
    and I am rocking . . .
        rocking . . .
            like a boat
            in the waves
                of her song.

DEBORAH CHANDRA

Sing Me Strong

Kiss me a story
Dance me a song
Sing to me, Daddy
Sing me strong

Drum me a rhythm
Clap me a rhyme
Play for me, Daddy
Play me fine

Snap me a finger
Tap me a toe
Twirl me dizzy
Hold me slow

Whistle me silly
Dance till dawn
Laugh with me, Daddy
Laugh me long

Spin me a secret
Tap my heartbeat
Talk to me, Daddy
Whisper me sweet

Hum me some jazz notes
Cry me the blues
Trill me your saxophone
Rock me true

Dance, my Daddy
Dance me to sleep
Dance me a sweet dream
Dance me deep

MEGAN MCDONALD

The Giant Seeker

Riding high
on daddy's shoulders,
bouncing in
and out of wind—
I reach for giants.
Playing hide and seek
with soft-skinned leaves
of summer
we glide across the lawn.
Daddy gallops on
through spiderwebs
of light and sky.

"Watch your head,"
he sings.

I am the giant seeker
on the back of a King.

REBECCA KAI DOTLICH

32

Dancing Nan

Dancing Nan!
Dancing Nan!
She's spinning around
as fast as she can.
She's skipping and jumping
she never sits down.
Oh, Dancing Nan
is a merry-go-round!
She's twisting and twirling
over the chairs.
She's bouncing and flouncing
up and down stairs.
Nan's my best friend,
though she never stays still;
I love her a lot,
and I always will
as she zips through the halls
almost too fast to see—
I just wish
she'd
slow
down
and come play with me.

SUSAN HART LINDQUIST

You and Me

Listen to the baby laugh!

When I was a baby, I did that.

His skin's so soft. His hair's so fine.

I know my numbers up to nine.

See how high he kicks his feet?

Yesterday I lost two teeth.

Grandma says he's sweet as jam.

Look and see how tall I am.

He looks just like a little elf.

I can tie all by myself.

Shhh . . . he's finally sleeping, see?

Hurray! It's time for you and me!

REBECCA KAI DOTLICH

My Baby Brother

My baby brother's beautiful,
So perfect and so tiny.
His skin is soft and velvet brown;
His eyes are dark and shiny.

His hair is black and curled up tight;
His two new teeth are sharp and white.
I like it when he chews his toes;
And when he laughs, his dimple shows.

Mary Ann Hoberman

Grandma's Lap

Come.
Climb on Grandma's knee.
Curl up in my lap.
Bring a book to share with me
Before we take our nap.
We'll read and rock and rock and read
Until we start to doze.
Then, with my arms held round you tight,
We'll let our eyelids softly close.

JOY N. HULME

Worlds of Make-Believe

Elf Folk Frolic

We are elf folk, small and merry,
    Apple-cheeked and dumpling round.
Acorn-capped and petal-vested,
    So we troop along the ground.

We step lively through the flowers
    In a column, two by two,
As the daisies nod and kiss us
    With a drop of morning dew.

CONSTANCE ANDREA KEREMES

The Little Elfman

I met a little Elfman once,
    Down where the lilies blow.
I asked him why he was so small,
    And why he didn't grow.

He slightly frowned, and with his eye
    He looked me through and through—
"I'm just as big for me," said he,
    "As you are big for you."

JOHN KENDRICK BANGS

The Gnome

One warm summer night
When I hurried home
By the edge of the woods
I saw a gnome.
He wore a red pointy cap
And a tidy blue coat;
His beard was white
Like an old Billy goat.
He was chubby and round
And not very tall,
But his voice was loud
For a creature so small.
He sang as he went—
A fiddler's tune—
And I followed him there
By the light of the moon.

I walked on my tiptoes
And kept out of sight
As I tracked the gnome
In the darkening night
To a strange little house
In a hollow tree.
Then I stepped on a branch—
He knew it was me!
He turned, looked up,
And just as I feared,
With a blink of an eye
He . . . disappeared!

LILLIAN M. FISHER

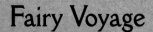

Fairy Voyage

If I were just a fairy small,
I'd take a leaf and sail away,
I'd sit astride the stem and guide
It straight to Fairyland—and stay.

ANONYMOUS

Forest Fairy

She tiptoes in
and out of sight;
a forest princess
in the night,
to sing her songs
to butterflies,
while tucking in
the dragonflies.
She dances through
the emerald weeds,
sprinkling violet
flower seeds;
planting secrets;
wishes too—

those are things that fairies do.

REBECCA KAI DOTLICH

FROM **Peter Pan**

Whenever a child says,
"I don't believe in fairies,"
there's a little fairy somewhere
that falls right down dead.

SIR JAMES M. BARRIE

As Long as You Know How to Dream

Adrift on an ocean of bottomless joy,
    My ship is a strawberry leaf,
My only companions, a mermaid or two
    Who live on an amethyst reef.

We all collect sunshine in amber tureens,
    And sell it a penny a pound
To fresh-water nymphs who mix it with dreams
    And scatter it freely around.

Would you like to come sail with the mermaids and me,
    And breakfast on laughter and cream?
There's room for us all on my strawberry leaf
    As long as you know how to dream.

EVELYN AMUEDO WADE

Magic Story for Falling Asleep

When the last giant came out of his cave
and his bones turned into the mountain
and his clothes turned into the flowers,

nothing was left but his tooth
which my dad took home in his truck
which my granddad carved into a bed

which my mom tucks me into at night
when I dream of the last giant
when I fall asleep on the mountain.

NANCY WILLARD

It's Story Time!

The Quangle Wangle's Hat

I

On the top of the Crumpetty Tree
    The Quangle Wangle sat,
But his face you could not see,
    On account of his Beaver Hat.
For his Hat was a hundred and two feet wide,
With ribbons and bibbons on every side,
And bells, and buttons, and loops, and lace,
So that nobody ever could see the face
      Of the Quangle Wangle Quee.

II

The Quangle Wangle said
   To himself on the Crumpetty Tree,—
"Jam, and jelly, and bread
   Are the best of food for me!
But the longer I live on this Crumpetty Tree
The plainer than ever it seems to me
That very few people come this way
And that life on the whole is far from gay!"
         Said the Quangle Wangle Quee.

III

But there came to the Crumpetty Tree,
   Mr. and Mrs. Canary;
And they said,—"Did ever you see
   Any spot so charmingly airy?
May we build a nest on your lovely Hat?
Mr. Quangle Wangle, grant us that!
O please let us come and build a nest
Of whatever material suits you best,
         Mr. Quangle Wangle Quee!"

IV

And besides, to the Crumpetty Tree
   Came the Stork, the Duck, and the Owl;
The Snail, and the Bumble-Bee,
   The Frog, and the Fimble Fowl;
(The Fimble Fowl, with a Corkscrew leg;)
And all of them said,—"We humbly beg,
We may build our homes on your lovely Hat,—
Mr. Quangle Wangle, grant us that!
     Mr. Quangle Wangle Quee!"

V

And the Golden Grouse came there,
   And the Pobble who has no toes,—
And the small Olympian bear,—
   And the Dong with a luminous nose.
And the Blue Baboon, who played the flute,—
And the Orient Calf from the Land of Tute,—
And the Attery Squash, and the Bisky Bat,—
All came and built on the lovely Hat
     Of the Quangle Wangle Quee.

VI

And the Quangle Wangle said
   To himself on the Crumpetty Tree,—
"When all these creatures move
   What a wonderful noise there'll be."
And at night by the light of the Mulberry moon
They danced to the Flute of the Blue Baboon,
On the broad green leaves of the Crumpetty Tree.
And all were as happy as happy could be,
     With the Quangle Wangle Quee.

EDWARD LEAR

Jabberwocky

'Twas brillig, and the slithy toves
  Did gyre and gimble in the wabe:
All mimsy were the borogoves,
  And the mome raths outgrabe.

"Beware the Jabberwock, my son!
  The jaws that bite, the claws that catch!
Beware the Jubjub bird, and shun
  The frumious Bandersnatch!"

He took his vorpal sword in hand:
  Long time the manxome foe he sought—
So rested he by the Tumtum tree,
  And stood awhile in thought.

And as in uffish thought he stood,
  The Jabberwock, with eyes of flame,
Came whiffling through the tulgey wood,
  And burbled as it came!

One, two! One, two! And through and through
  The vorpal blade went snicker-snack!
He left it dead, and with its head
  He went galumphing back.

"And hast thou slain the Jabberwock?
  Come to my arms, my beamish boy!
O frabjous day! Callooh! Callay!"
  He chortled in his joy.

'Twas brillig, and the slithy toves
  Did gyre and gimble in the wabe:
All mimsy were the borogoves,
  And the mome raths outgrabe.

LEWIS CARROLL

Three Wise Old Women

Three wise old women were they, were they,
Who went to walk on a winter day:
One carried a basket to hold some berries,
One carried a ladder to climb for berries,
The third, and she was the wisest one,
Carried a fan to keep off the sun.

But they went so far, and they went so fast,
They quite forgot their way at last,
So one of the wise women cried in a fright,
"Suppose we should meet a bear tonight!
Suppose he should eat me!"

"And me!!"
"And me!!"

"What is to be done?" cried all the three.

"Dear, dear!" said one. "We'll climb a tree,
Then out of the way of the bears we'll be."
But there wasn't a tree for miles around;
They were too frightened to stay on the ground,
So they climbed their ladder up to the top,
And sat there screaming, "We'll drop! We'll drop!"

But the wind was as strong as wind could be,
And blew their ladder right out to sea;
So the three wise women were all afloat
In a leaky ladder instead of a boat,
And every time the waves rolled in,
Of course the poor things were wet to the skin.

Then they took their basket, the water to bale,
They put up their fan instead of a sail:
But what became of the wise women then,
Whether they ever sailed home again,
Whether they saw any bears, or no,
You must find out, for I don't know.

Elizabeth T. Corbett

Wynken, Blynken, and Nod

Wynken, Blynken, and Nod one night
    Sailed off in a wooden shoe—
Sailed on a river of crystal light,
    Into a sea of dew.
"Where are you going, and what do you wish?"
    The old moon asked the three.
"We have come to fish for the herring fish
That live in this beautiful sea;
Nets of silver and gold have we!"
    Said Wynken,
    Blynken,
    And Nod.

The old moon laughed and sang a song,
    As they rocked in the wooden shoe,
And the wind that sped them all night long
    Ruffled the waves of dew.
The little stars were the herring fish
    That lived in that beautiful sea—
"Now cast your nets wherever you wish—
Never afeared are we";
So cried the stars to the fishermen three:
    Wynken,
    Blynken,
    And Nod.

All night long their nets they threw
    To the stars in the twinkling foam—
Then down from the skies came the wooden shoe,
    Bringing the fishermen home;
'Twas all so pretty a sail it seemed
    As if it could not be,
And some folks thought 'twas a dream they'd dreamed
Of sailing that beautiful sea—
But I shall name you the fishermen three:
        Wynken,
        Blynken,
        And Nod.

Wynken and Blynken are two little eyes,
    And Nod is a little head,
And the wooden shoe that sailed the skies
    Is the wee one's trundle-bed.
So shut your eyes while mother sings
    Of wonderful sights that be,
And you shall see the beautiful things
As you rock in the misty sea,
Where the old shoe rocked the fishermen three:
        Wynken,
        Blynken,
        And Nod.

EUGENE FIELD

Little Hands
and Fingers—
Little Toes
and Feet

Ten Little Fingers

You have ten little fingers.
They all belong to you.
What can you do with them?
What can you do with them?

You can close them up tight.
Open them wide.
Put them together.
Make them all hide.

Make them leap high.
Make them fall low.
And fold them so gently
And sit just so.

TRADITIONAL

Up to the Ceiling

Your hands can reach up to the ceiling.
Your hands can fall down to the floor.

One hand can point left to the window.
One hand can point right to the door.

This is your right hand—
Raise it up high.

This is your left hand—
Reach for the sky.

Right hand, left hand,
Turn them around.

Left hand, right hand.
Pound, pound, pound.

TRADITIONAL

Eentsy, Weentsy Spider

Eentsy, weentsy spider
Climbed up the waterspout.

Down poured the rain
And washed the spider out.

Out came the shining sun
And dried up all the rain.

And eentsy, weentsy spider
Climbed up the spout again.

TRADITIONAL

Five Great Big Dinosaurs

Five great big dinosaurs
All began to roar.
One sped away—
Then there were four.

Four great big dinosaurs
Stood beneath a tree.
One sped away—
Then there were three.

Three great big dinosaurs
All began to chew.
One got tired and went away—
Then there were two.

Two great big dinosaurs
Sat in the sun.
One ran to catch its tail—
Then there was one.

One great big dinosaur
Stood alone not having any fun.
Until it ran to find its friends—

Then there were none.

TRADITIONAL
RETOLD BY LEE BENNETT HOPKINS

This Little Piggy

1

This little piggy went to market.
This little piggy stayed home.
This little piggy had roast beef.
This little piggy had none.

2

And this little piggy cried:

3

"Wee, wee,
Wee, wee,
Wee, wee,
Wee, WHEE,"

4

All the way home!

5

TRADITIONAL

Good Night

Evening Is Coming

The evening is coming, the sun sinks to rest,
The birds are all flying straight home to their nests,
"Caw, caw," says the crow as he flies overhead,
It's time little children were going to bed.

Here comes the pony, his work is all done,
Down through the meadow he takes a good run,
Up go his heels—and down goes his head.
It's time little children were going to bed.

ANONYMOUS

Sleepy Head

Goodnight, goodnight, my sleepy head,
Kiss your Daddy, then off to bed.
I'll give you one last tucking in,
It's time for dreaming to begin.

PAM SMALLCOMB

How Come?

How come
the moon
is big enough
to light my room,
yet small enough
to hide behind
my thumb?

How come
your smile
is small enough
to fit your face,
yet big enough
to light
the darkest place?

Cynthia Pederson

Lullaby

Flowers are closed and lambs are sleeping;
Lullaby, oh, lullaby!
Stars are up, the moon is peeping;
Lullaby, oh, lullaby!

While the birds are silence keeping,
Lullaby, oh, lullaby!
Sleep, my baby, fall a-sleeping,
Lullaby, oh, lullaby!

CHRISTINA G. ROSSETTI

The House Is Sleeping

The house is sleeping
    She has closed her eyes
Dark are her windows
    Dark are the skies
The streets are silent
    And empty of cars
High in the heavens
    The winking of stars
Sprinkle their stardust
    On valley and hill
While everyone, everything's
    Sleeping and still
The whole world is sleeping
    Even you!

I'll pull up the covers, now,
    And go to sleep, too.

LILLIAN M. FISHER

Night

Rests
on
shadows.

Kisses
my
eyes.

Dips
me
in twilight.

Covers
me
with dreams.

C. DREW LAMM

Lullaby

Night
> comes

to whisper
> in my ear

dream songs
> no one else

can hear.

SUSAN HART LINDQUIST

FROM How to Sing or Read

So when the night is come, and you have gone to bed,
All the songs you love to sing shall echo in
    your head.

ROBERT LOUIS STEVENSON

Index of Titles

Index of First Lines

Index of Authors

Acknowledgments

Every effort has been made to trace the ownership of all copyrighted material and to secure necessary permissions to reprint these selections. In the event of any question arising to the use of any material, the editor and the publisher, while expressing regret for any inadvertent error, will be happy to make the necessary correction in future printings. Thanks are due to the following for permission to reprint the selections below:

Curtis Brown, Ltd. for "Five Great Big Dinosaurs" by Lee Bennett Hopkins. Copyright © 1998 by Lee Bennett Hopkins; "My Name" by Lee Bennett Hopkins, Copyright © 1974 by Lee Bennett Hopkins, originally published in *Kim's Place and Other Poems* (Henry Holt); "Toy Telephone" by Lee Bennett Hopkins. Copyright © 1972 by Lee Bennett Hopkins, originally published in *Charlie's World* (Bobbs-Merrill); "Quiet Morning" by Karen Winnick. Copyright © 1998 by Karen Winnick. All printed by permission of Curtis Brown, Ltd.

Rebecca Kai Dotlich for "Forest Fairy," "The Giant Seeker," "My Secret Step," and "You and Me." Used by permission of the author, who controls all rights.

Farrar, Straus & Giroux, Inc. for "Mama's Song" and "Tent" from *Balloons and Other Poems* by Deborah Chandra. Copyright © 1990 by Deborah Chandra. Reprinted by permission of Farrar, Straus & Giroux, Inc.

Lillian M. Fisher for "The Gnome" and "The House Is Sleeping." Used by permission of the author, who controls all rights.

Fran Haraway for "A Place of My Own." Used by permission of the author, who controls all rights.

Lee Bennett Hopkins for "And There" by Prince Redcloud. Used by permission of Lee Bennett Hopkins for the author, who controls all rights.

Joy N. Hulme for "Grandma's Lap." Used by permission of the author, who controls all rights.

Constance Andrea Keremes for "Elf Folk Frolic." Used by permission of the author, who controls all rights.

Karla Kuskin for "Comfortable Old Chair." Copyright © 1992 by Karla Kuskin. Used by permission of the author, who controls all rights.

C. Drew Lamm for "Night." Used by permission of the author, who controls all rights.

Susan Hart Lindquist for "Dancing Nan" and "Lullaby." Used by permission of the author, who controls all rights.

Little, Brown & Company for "This Is My Rock" from *One at a Time* by David McCord. Copyright © 1929 by David McCord. "My Baby Brother" from *Fathers, Mothers, Sisters, Brothers* by Mary Ann Hoberman. Text copyright © 1991 by Mary Ann Hoberman; illustrations copyright © 1991 by Marylin Hafner. Both reprinted by permission of Little, Brown & Company.

Megan McDonald for "Sing Me Strong." Used by permission of the author, who controls all rights.

Beverly McLoughland for "How to Talk to Your Snowman." Used by permission of the author, who controls all rights.

G. P. Putnam's Sons for "Everybody Says" from *Everything and Anything* by Dorothy Aldis, copyright 1925–1927; copyright renewed 1953–1955 by Dorothy Aldis. "Bursting," "The Secret Place" and "See, I Can Do It" from *All Together* by Dorothy Aldis, copyright 1925–1928, 1934, 1939, 1952, copyright renewed 1953–1956, 1962, 1967 by Dorothy Aldis. All reprinted by permission of G.P. Putnam's Sons.

Marian Reiner for "How Come?" by Cynthia Pederson. Copyright © 1998 by Cynthia Pederson. Used by permission of Marian Reiner for the author.

Pam Smallcomb for "Sleepy Head." Used by permission of the author, who controls all rights.

Evelyn Amuedo Wade for "As Long as You Know How to Dream." Used by permission of the author, who controls all rights.

Nancy Willard for "Magic Story for Falling Asleep." Copyright © 1978 by Nancy Willard.

Charlotte Zolotow for "People." Used by permission of the author, who controls all rights.

To my sister—Donna Lea Venturi—
who climbed into my lap—and life!

—L. B. H.

To Bette Schmitt

—K. B.

SIMON & SCHUSTER BOOKS FOR YOUNG READERS An imprint of Simon & Schuster Children's Publishing Division 1230 Avenue of the Americas, New York, New York 10020. Text copyright © 1998 by Lee Bennett Hopkins. Illustrations copyright © 1998 by Kathryn Brown. For additional copyright details, see page 79. All rights reserved including the right of reproduction in whole or in part in any form. SIMON & SCHUSTER BOOKS FOR YOUNG READERS is a trademark of Simon & Schuster. Book design by Paul Zakris. The text for this book is set in 16-point Shannon Book. The illustrations are rendered in watercolor. Printed in Hong Kong.
First Edition
10 9 8 7 6 5 4 3 2 1

LIBRARY OF CONGRESS CATALOGING-IN-PUBLICATION DATA

Climb into my lap : poems to read together / selected by Lee Bennett Hopkins ; illustrated by Kathryn Brown.

    p.   cm.

    Includes index.

    Summary: A collection of poems chosen to be read aloud, by such authors as Edward Lear, Charlotte Zolotow, and Nancy Willard.

    ISBN 0-689-80715-5 (hardcover)

    1. Children's poetry, American. 2. Children's poetry, English. [1. American poetry—Collections. 2. English poetry—Collections.] I. Hopkins, Lee Bennett. II. Brown, Kathryn, 1955– ill.

PS586.3.C58 1998

811.008'09282—dc21

97-18670